First published in 2019 by Untold Books

www.untoldbooks.com
Text copyright © 2019 Darren Garwood
Illustration copyright © 2019 Carl Osborne
ISBN: 978-1-5272-4605-8

# Jackson's Solution
# to Pollution

Words by Darren Garwood
Illustrations by Carl Osborne

UNTOLD BOOKS

Dad gives me a kiss and says goodnight.
He's barely out of my door and I'm off on a flight.

I fly so quick that my hair is blowing.
The sun is hot here, I feel like I'm glowing.

I see a desert island, what a great place to rest.
But as I get closer the island's not at its best.

The shoreline's a mess,
all scattered with litter.

A crab on the beach yells,
"I'd clean it myself, if I was a bit fitter."

I say, "I'll clean up this rubbish and plastic."

The crab replies, "Jackson,
that would be fantastic."

But I look out to sea as a big wave comes along.
More rubbish is washed up, this is all so wrong.

There's metal and plastic and an old baby's cot.
This is not just a little. This is really a lot!

So I open my mouth and yell really loud,
"Gather together, sea creatures, please form a crowd."

Hundreds of creatures
lift their heads from the waves.

Two mermaids come out
of the old smugglers' caves.

"Hello," I say. "Please listen," I shout.
"Because I'm going to clean this pollution right out."

"Please pick up the little ones and those who can't swim.
Hold onto something, everyone, so I can begin."

I take a deep breath and suck up the sea.
In one large gulp it is now pollution free.

I swallow all the rubbish, including a bolt.
I dribble the sea back and sneeze out the salt.

The sea is now clean and free from pollution.
The island's still dirty, but I have a solution.

The shoreline and island are still in a mess,
"Let's work together on this great cleaning quest."

The mermaids slide elegantly onto the shore.
"We want to help," they shout. "We can't bear this no more."

An army of crabs march along the sand.
All together they yell, "We'll lend you a hand."

A team of moles poke their heads from the ground.
"Can we help, please? We need room for our mounds."


"Of course," I say. "That would be great.
Let's get cleaning before it's too late."

Standing behind me there are hundreds of helpers.
Geckos, frogs and meerkats climb out of their shelters.

They all form a chain to pass on the junk,
with a crash and a wallop and a clink and a clunk.

A frog shouts, "The island's now clean, this is fantastic.
But what do we do with this big pile of plastic?"

So I take a deep breath and suck up the pile.
I swallow the fridge and the plastic, there's even a tile.

"The island is now clean and looking delightful,
To keep it this way you must start to recycle."

The fish and the whales jump out of the sea.
"Please, Jackson," they cheer,
"won't you stay for tea?"

"I'm sorry, I can't, my belly is full.
If I eat any more, I couldn't fly at all."

So I lie on the sand for a well-deserved rest.
When I wake up, I'm huddled up on dad's chest.

And he's telling me an amazing story
about a great cleaning quest.

Jackson Superhero might not be a real name, but it is a story about a real boy, and as the name suggests, Jackson is far from ordinary.

From birth, the real Jackson was like every other child. He passed all the regular milestones like talking, eating by himself and generally enjoying life. But just after his first birthday Jackson started to lose key skills. This is when he was diagnosed with Krabbe disease and wasn't expected to live beyond the age of two.

By mustering all his strength, and with a lot of love from his mum and dad, Jackson is still doing well at age five. The moral of the story is that while he may be limited during the day, in the evening, when he dreams, Jackson can be anything he wants to be.

We believe this fantastic story of a young boy going above and beyond will bring inspiration to parents and children who, for one reason or another, have to muster their superpowers on a daily basis. This book is for those who have to push back against daily challenges, for whom comfort and happiness requires extra patience, strength and love. Just as importantly, it's for those who rely on the support and inspiration of others. No matter what kind of day you are having, we believe this book will still make you smile.

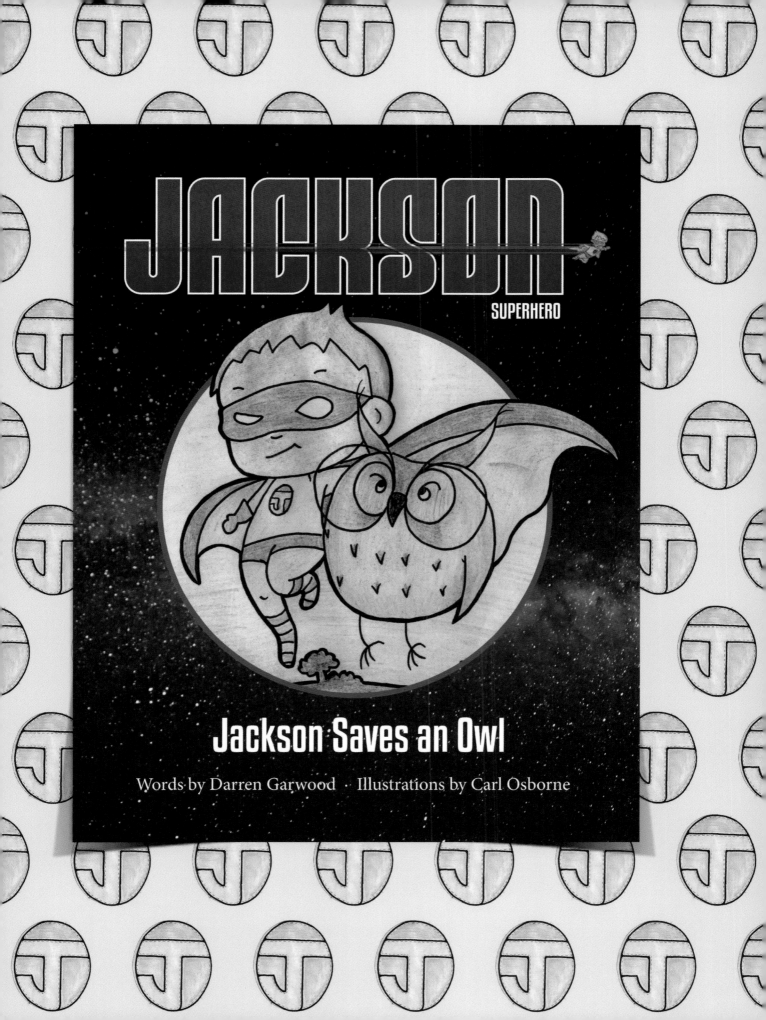

Printed in Great Britain
by Amazon